RUS

BOND

Tales from the Childhood

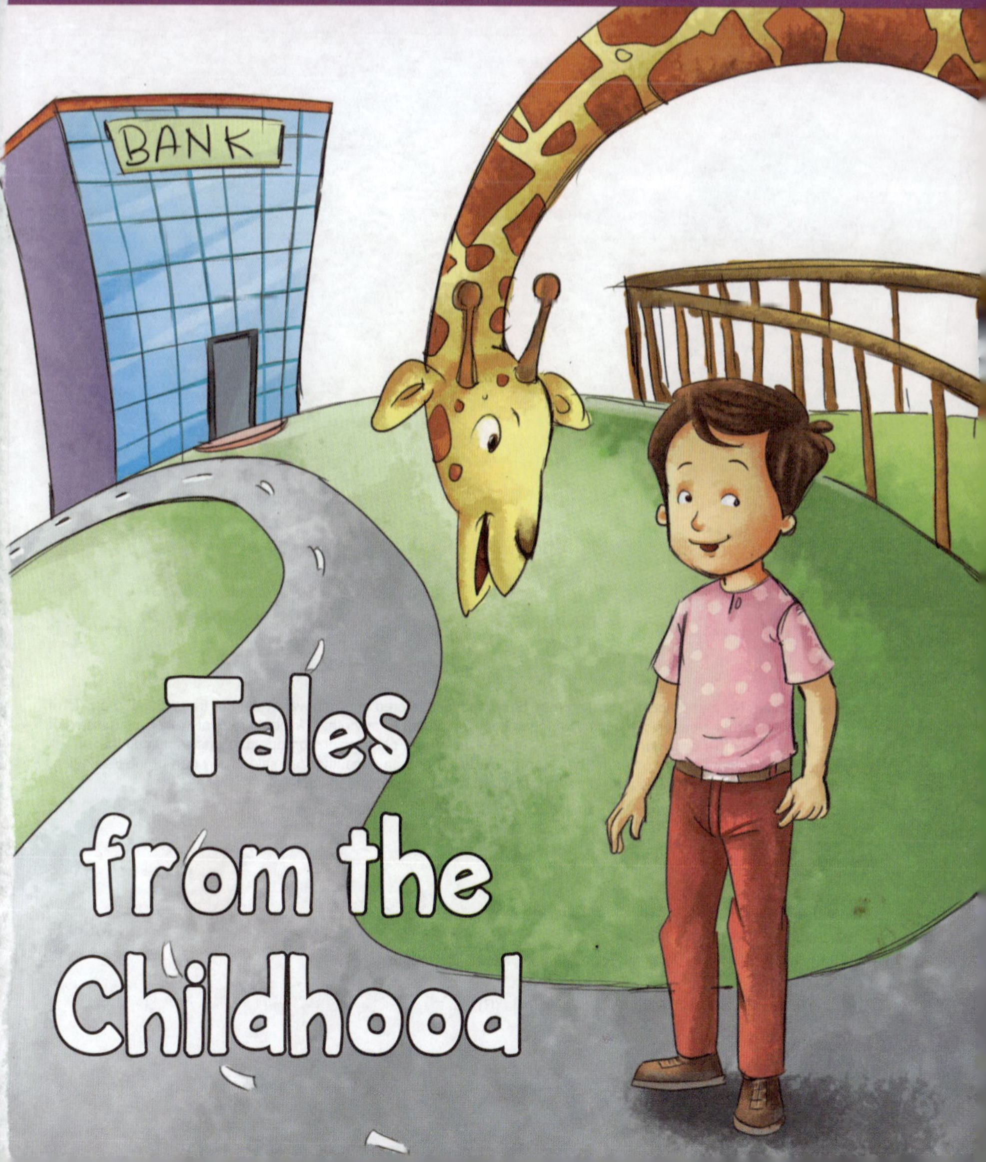

B. Jain Publishers (P) Ltd.
D-157, Sector 63, Noida - 201307, U.P
Registered office: 1921/10, Chuna Mandi, Paharganj, New Delhi-110055

Published in arrangement with Rupa Publications India (P) Ltd.

Printed in India

Mukesh Starts a Zoo

On a visit to Delhi with his parents, Mukesh spent two crowded hours at the zoo. He was dazzled by the many colourful birds, fascinated by the reptiles, charmed by the gibbons and chimps, and awestruck by the big cats—the lions, tigers and leopards. There was no zoo in the small town of Dehra where he lived, and the jungle was some way across the river-bed. So, as soon as he got home, he decided that he would have a zoo of his own.

'I'm going to start a zoo,' he announced at breakfast, the day after his return.
'But you don't have any birds or animals,' said Dolly, his little sister.
'I'll soon find them,' said Mukesh. 'That's what a zoo is all about—collecting animals.'

He was gazing at the white-washed walls of the verandah, where a gecko, a small wall lizard, was in pursuit of a fly. A little later Mukesh was trying to catch the lizard. But it was more alert than it

looked, and always managed to keep a few inches ahead of his grasp.

'That's not the way to catch a lizard,' said Teju, appearing on the verandah steps. Teju and his sister Koki lived next door.

'You catch it, then,' said Mukesh.

Teju fetched a stick from the garden, where it had been used to prop up sweet-peas. He used the stick to tip the lizard off the wall and into a shoe-box.

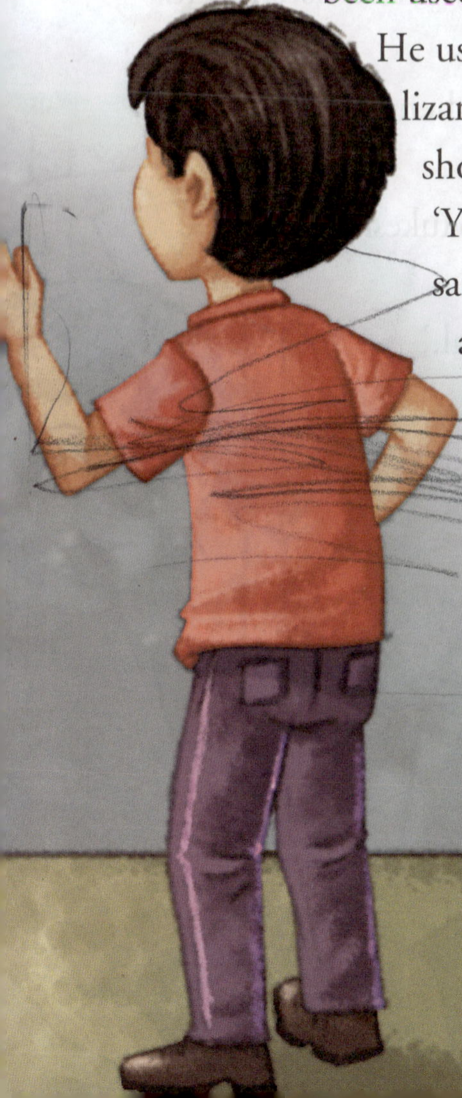

'You'll be my Head Keeper,' said Mukesh, and soon he and Teju were at work in the back garden setting up enclosures with a roll of wire-netting they had found in the poultry shed.

'What else can we have in the zoo?' asked Teju. 'We need more than a lizard.'

'There's your grandmother's parrot,' said Mukesh.

'That's a good idea. But we won't tell her about it—not yet. I don't think she'd lend it to us. You see, it's a religious parrot. She's taught it lots of prayers and chants.'

'Then people are sure to come and listen to it. They'll pay, too.'

'We must have the parrot, then. What else?'

'Well, there's my dog,' said Mukesh. 'He's very fierce.'

'But a dog isn't a zoo animal.'

'Mine is—he's a wild dog. Look, he's black all over and he's got yellow eyes.

There's no other dog like him.'

Mukesh's dog, who spent most of his time sleeping on the verandah, raised his head and obligingly revealed his yellow eyes.

'He's got jaundice,' said Teju.

'They've always been yellow.'

'All right, then, we've got a lizard, a parrot and a black dog with yellow eyes.' 'Koki has a white rabbit. Will she lend it to us?'

'I don't know. She thinks a lot of her rabbit. Maybe we can rent it from her.'

'And there's Sitaram's donkey.'

Sitaram, the dhobi-boy, usually used a donkey to deliver and collect the laundry from the houses along this particular street.

'Do you really want a donkey?' asked Teju doubtfully.

'Why not? It's a wild donkey. Haven't you heard of them?'

'I've heard of a wild ass, but not a wild donkey.'

'Well, they're all related to each other—asses, donkeys and mules.'

'Why don't you paint black stripes on it and call it a zebra?'

'No, that's cheating. It's got to be a proper zoo. No tricks—it's not a circus!'

On Saturday afternoon, a large placard with corrected spelling announced the opening of the zoo. It hung from the branches of the jack-fruit tree. Children were allowed in free but grown-ups had to buy tickets at fifty paise each, and Koki and Dolly were selling home-made tickets to the occasional passer-by or parent who happened to look in. Mukesh and his friends had worked hard at making notices for the various enclosures and each resident of the zoo was appropriately named.

The first attraction was a large packing-case filled with an assortment of house-lizards. They looked rather sluggish, having been generously fed with a supply of beetles and other insects.

Then came an enclosure in which Koki's white rabbit was on display. Freshly washed and brushed, it looked very cuddly and was praised by all.

Staring at it with evil intent from behind wire-netting was Mukesh's dog—RARE BLACK DOG WITH YELLOW EYES read the notice. Those yellow eyes were now trying hard to hypnotise the pink eyes of Koki's nervous rabbit. The dog pawed at the ground, trying to dig its way out from under the fence to get at the rabbit.

Tethered to a mango tree was Sitaram's small donkey. And tacked to the tree was a placard saying WILD ASS FROM KUTCH. A distant relative it may have been, but everyone recognised it as the local washerman's beast of burden. Every now and then it tried to break loose, for it was long past its feeding time.

There was also a duck that did not seem to belong to anyone, and a small cow that had strayed in on its own; but the star attraction was the parrot. As it could recite three different prayers, over and over again, it was soon surrounded by a group of admiring parents, all of whom wished they had a parrot who could pray, or rather, do their praying for them. Oddly enough, Koki's grandmother had chosen that day for visiting the temple, so she was unaware of the fuss that was being made of her pet, or even that it had been made an honorary member of the zoo. Teju had convinced himself she wouldn't mind. While Mukesh and Teju were escorting visitors around the zoo, lecturing them on wild dogs and wild asses, Koki and Dolly were doing a brisk trade at the ticket counter. They had collected about ten rupees and were hoping for yet more, when there was a disturbance in the enclosures.

The black dog with yellow eyes had finally managed to dig his way out of his cage, and was now busy trying to dig his way into the rabbit's compartment. The rabbit was running round and round in panic-stricken circles. Meanwhile, the donkey had finally snapped the rope that held it and, braying loudly, scattered the spectators and made for home.

Koki went to the rescue of her rabbit and soon had it cradled in her arms. The dog now turned his attention to the duck. The duck flew over the packing-case, while the dog landed in it, scattering lizards in all directions.

In all this confusion, no one noticed that the door of the parrot's cage had slipped open. With a squawk and a whirr of wings, the bird shot out of the cage and flew off into a nearby orchard.

'The parrot's gone!' shouted Dolly, and almost immediately a silence fell upon the assembled visitors and children. Even the dog stopped barking.

Granny's praying parrot had escaped! How could they possibly face her? Teju wondered if she would believe him if he told her it had flown off to heaven.

'Can anyone see it?' he asked tearfully.

'It's in a mango tree,' said Dolly. 'It won't come back.'

The crowd fell away, unwilling to share any of the blame when Koki's grandmother came home and discovered what had happened. 'What are we going to do now?' asked Teju, looking to Koki for help; but Koki was too upset to suggest anything. Mukesh had an idea.

'I know!' he said. 'We'll get another one!'

'How?'

'Well, there's the ten rupees we've collected. We can buy a new parrot for ten rupees!'

'But won't Granny know the difference?' asked Teju.

'All these hill parrots look alike,' said Mukesh.

So, taking the cage with them, they hurried off to the bazaar, where they soon found a bird-seller who was happy to sell them a parrot not unlike Granny's. He assured them it would talk.

'It looks like your grandmother's parrot,' said Mukesh on the way home. 'But can it pray?'

'Of course not,' said Koki. 'But we can teach it.'

Koki's grandmother, who was short-sighted, did not notice the substitution; but she complained bitterly that the bird had stopped repeating its prayers and was instead making rude noises and even swearing occasionally.

Teju soon remedied this sad state of affairs. Every morning he stood in front of the parrot's cage and repeated Granny's prayers. Within a few weeks the bird had learnt to repeat one of them. Granny was happy again—not only because her parrot had started praying once more, but because Teju had started praying too!

The Boy Who Broke the Bank

Nathu, the sweeper-boy, grumbled to himself as he swept the steps of a small local bank, owned for the most part by Seth Govind Ram, a man of wealth whose haphazard business dealings had often brought him to the verge of ruin. Nathu used the small broom hurriedly and carelessly; the dust, after rising in a cloud above his head, settled down again on the steps. As Nathu was banging his pan against a dustbin,

Sitaram, the washerman's son, passed by.
Sitaram was on his delivery round. He had a bundle of pressed clothes balanced on his head.
'Don't raise such a dust!' he called out to Nathu.
'Are you annoyed because they are still refusing to pay you another five rupees a month?'

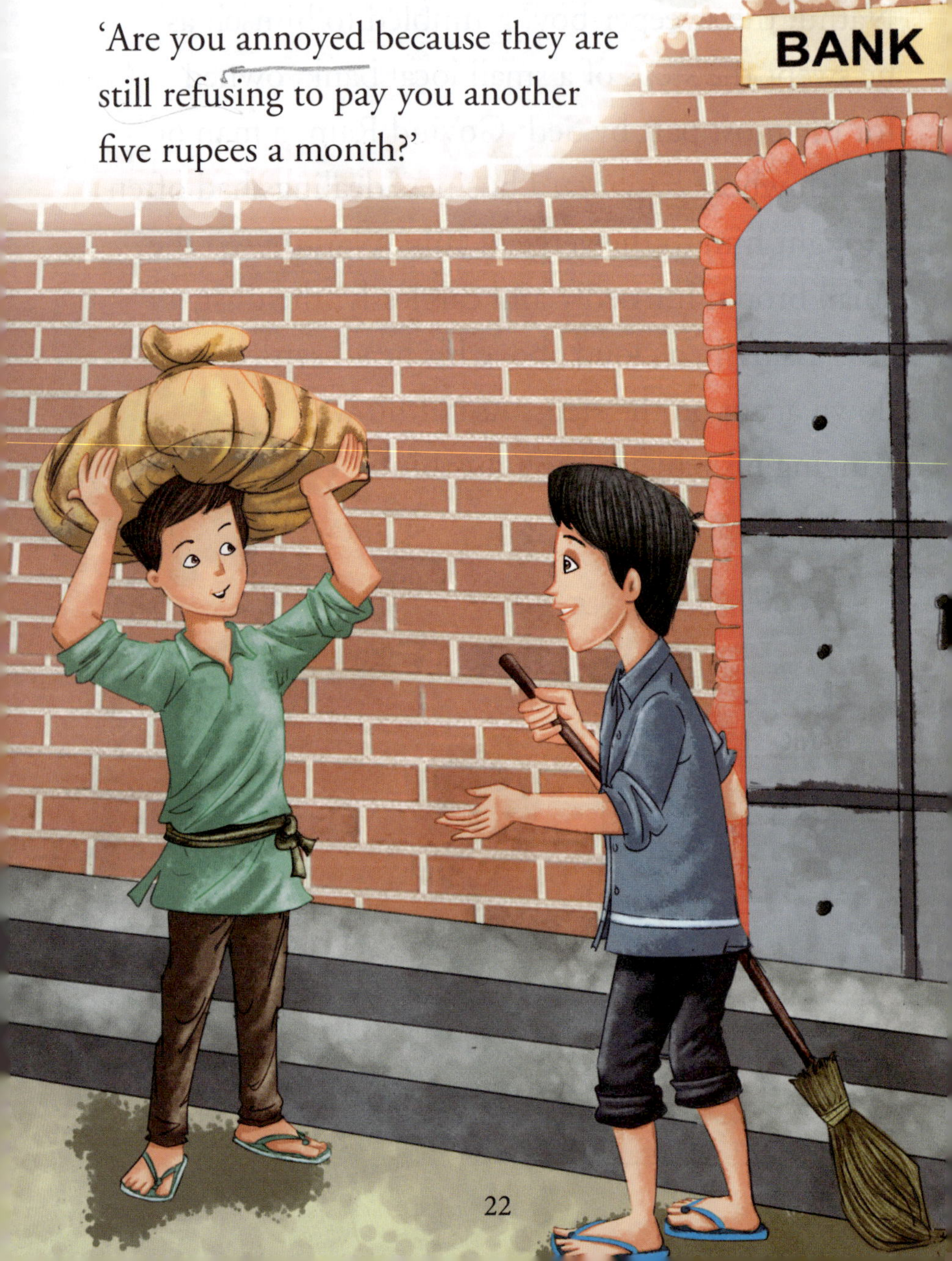

'I don't want to talk about it,' complained the sweeper-boy. 'I haven't even received my regular pay. And this is the end of the month. Soon two months' pay will be due. Who would think this was a bank, holding up a poor man's salary? As soon as I get my money, I'm off! Not another week will I work in the place.'

And Nathu banged his pan against the dustbin two or three times more, just to emphasise his point and give himself confidence.

'Well, I wish you luck,' said Sitaram. 'I'll be on the look-out for a new job for you.' And he plodded barefoot along the road, the big bundle of clothes hiding most of his head and shoulders.

At the fourth house he visited, delivering the washing, Sitaram overheard the woman of the house saying how difficult it was to get someone to sweep the courtyard. Tying up his bundle, Sitaram said: 'I know a sweeper-boy who's looking for work. He might be able to work for you from next month. He's with Seth Govind Ram's bank just now, but they are not giving him his pay, and he wants to leave.'

'Oh, is that so?' said Mrs Prakash. 'And why aren't they paying him?'

'They must be short of money,' said Sitaram with a shrug.

Mrs Prakash laughed, 'Well, tell him to come and see me when he's free.'

Sitaram, glad that he had been of some service both to a friend and to a customer, hoisted his bag on his shoulders and went on his way.

Mrs Prakash had to do some shopping. She gave instructions to her maidservant with regard to the baby and told the cook what she wanted for lunch. Her husband worked for a large company, and they could keep servants and do things in style. Having given her orders, she set out for the bazaar to make her customary tour of the cloth shops. A large, shady tamarind tree grew near the clock tower, and it was here that Mrs Prakash found her friend, Mrs Bhushan, sheltering from the heat. Mrs Bhushan was fanning herself with a large peacock's feather. She complained that the summer was the hottest in the history of the town. She then showed Mrs Prakash a sample of the cloth she was going to buy, and for five minutes they discussed its shade, texture and design.

When they had exhausted the subject, Mrs Prakash said: 'Do you know, my dear, Seth Govind Ram's bank can't even pay its employees. Only this morning I heard a complaint from their sweeper-boy, who hasn't received his pay for two months!'

'It's disgraceful!' exclaimed Mrs Bhushan. 'If they can't pay their sweeper, they must be in a bad way. None of the others can be getting paid either.'

She left Mrs Prakash at the tamarind tree and went in search of her husband, who was found sitting under the fan in Jugal Kishore's electrical goods shop, playing cards with the owner.

'So there you are!' cried Mrs Bhushan. 'I've been looking for you for nearly an hour. Where did you disappear to?'

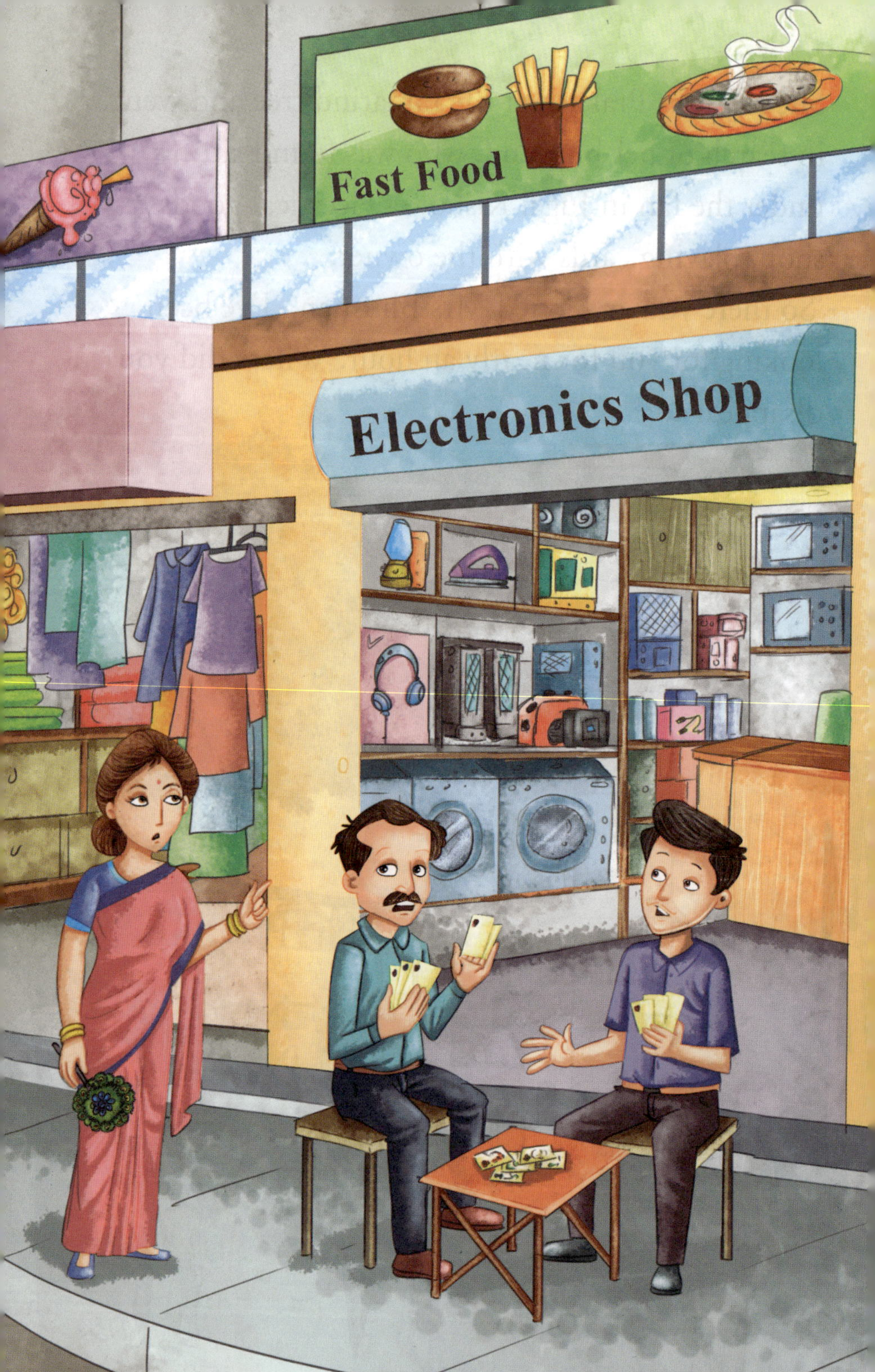
Fast Food
Electronics Shop

'Nowhere,' replied Mr Bhushan. 'Had you remained stationary in one shop, you might have found me. But you go from one to another, like a bee in a flower-garden.'

'Now don't start grumbling. The heat is bad enough. I don't know what's happening to this town. Even the bank is going bankrupt.'

'What did you say?' said Mr Jugal Kishore, sitting up suddenly. 'Which bank?'

'Why, Seth Govind Ram's bank, of course. I hear they've stopped paying their employees—no salary for over three months! Don't tell me you have an account with them, Mr Kishore?'

'No, but my neighbour has!' he said, and he called out to the keeper of the barber shop next door: 'Faiz Hussain, have you heard the latest? Seth Govind Ram's bank is about to collapse! You'd better take your money out while there's still time.'

Faiz Hussain, who was cutting the hair of an elderly gentleman, was so startled that his hand shook and he nicked his customer's ear. The customer yelped with pain and distress: pain, because of the cut, and distress, because of the awful news he had just heard. With one side of his neck still unshorn, he leapt out of his chair and sped across the road to a general merchant's store, where there was a telephone. He dialled Seth Govind Ram's number. The Seth was not at home. Where was he, then? The Seth was holidaying in Kashmir. Oh, was that so? The elderly gentleman did not believe it. He hurried back to the barber shop and told Faiz Hussain: 'The bird has flown! Seth Govind Ram has left town. Definitely, it means a collapse. I'll have the rest of my haircut another time.' And he dashed out of the shop and made a bee-line for his office and cheque book.

The news spread through the bazaar with the rapidity of a forest fire. From the general merchant's it travelled to the tea-shop, circulated amongst the customers, and then spread with them in various directions, to the paan-seller, the tailor, the fruit-vendor, the jeweller, the beggar sitting on the pavement .

Old Ganpat, the beggar, had a crooked leg and had been squatting on the pavement for years, calling for alms. In the evening someone would come with a barrow and take him away. He had never been known to walk. But now, on learning

that the bank was about to collapse, Ganpat astonished everyone by leaping to his feet and actually running at a good speed in the direction of the bank. It soon became known that he had well over a thousand rupees in savings.

Men stood in groups at street corners, discussing the situation. There hadn't been so much excitement since India last won a Test Match. The small town in the foot-hills seldom had a crisis, never had floods or earthquakes or droughts. And so the imminent crash of the local bank set everyone talking and speculating and rushing about in a frenzy.

Some boasted of their farsightedness, congratulating themselves on having taken out their money, or on never putting any in. Others speculated on the reasons for the crash, putting it all down to Seth Govind Ram's pleasure-loving ways. The Seth had fled the state, said one. He had fled the country, said another. He had a South American passport, said a third. Others insisted that he was hiding somewhere in the town. And there was a rumour that he had hanged himself from the tamarind tree, where he had been found that morning by the sweeper-boy.

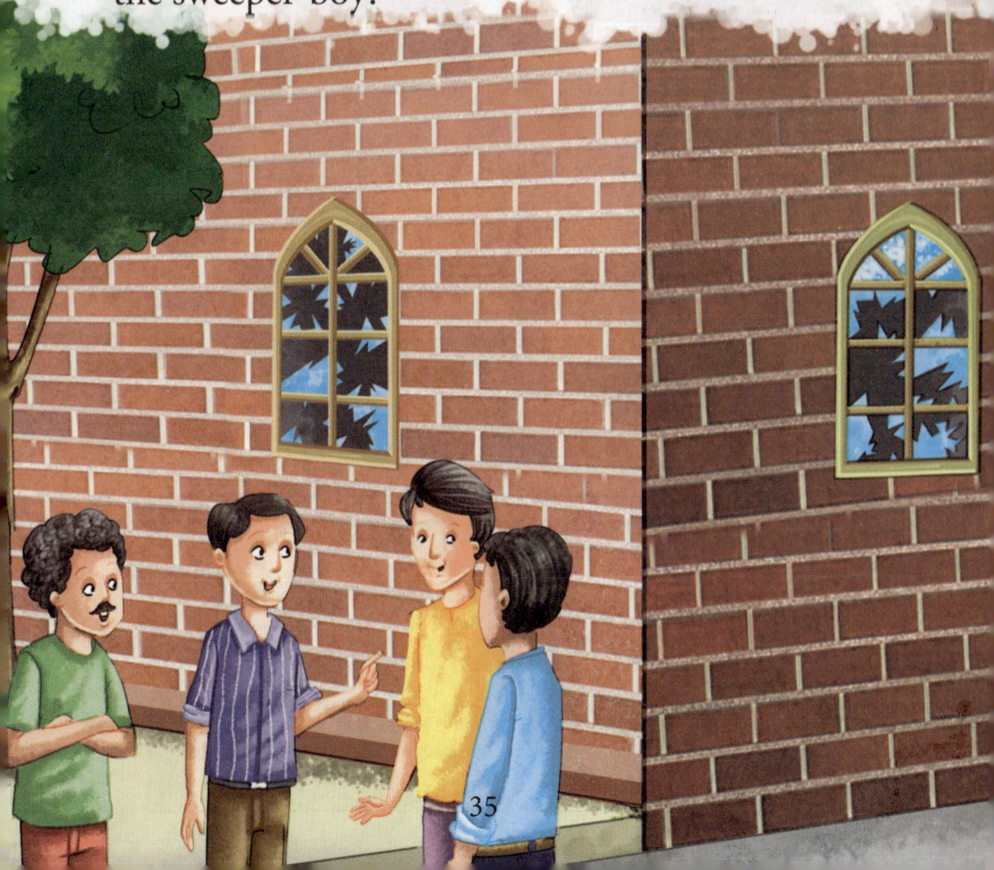

Someone who had a relative working as a clerk in the bank decided to phone him and get the facts. 'I don't know anything about it,' said the clerk, 'except that half the town is here, trying to take their money out. Everyone seems to have gone mad!' 'There's a rumour that none of you have been paid.'

'Well, all the clerks have had their salaries. We wouldn't be working otherwise. It may be that some of the part-time workers are getting paid late, but that isn't due to a shortage of money—only a few hundred rupees— it's just that the clerk who looks after their payments is on sick leave. You don't expect me to do his work, do you?' And he put the telephone down.

By afternoon the bank had gone through all its ready money, and the harassed manager was helpless. Emergency funds could only be obtained from one of the government banks, and now it was nearly closing time. He wasn't sure he could persuade the crowd outside to wait until the following morning. And Seth Govind Ram could be of no help from his luxury houseboat in Kashmir, five hundred miles away.

The clerks shut down their counters. But the people gathered outside on the steps of the bank, shouting: 'We want our money!' 'Give it to us today, break in!' 'Fetch Seth Govind Ram, we know he's hiding in the vaults!'

Mischief-makers, who did not have a paisa in the bank, joined the crowd. The manager stood at the door and tried to calm his angry customers. He declared that the bank had plenty of money, that they could withdraw all they wanted the following morning.

'We want it now!' chanted the people. 'Now, now, now!'

A few stones were thrown, and the manager retreated indoors, closing the iron-grilled gate.

A brick hurtled through the air and smashed into the plate-glass window which advertised the bank's assets.

Then the police arrived. They climbed the steps of the bank and, using their long sticks, pushed the crowd back until people began falling over each other. Gradually everyone dispersed, shouting that they would be back in the morning. Nathu arrived next morning to sweep the steps of the bank.
He saw the refuse and the broken glass and the stones

cluttering up the steps. Raising his hands in horror, he cried: 'Goondas! Hooligans! May they suffer from a thousand ills! It was bad enough being paid irregularly—now I must suffer an increase of work!' He smote the

steps with his broom, scattering the refuse.
'Good morning, Nathu,' said Sitaram, the washer-man's son, getting down from his bicycle. 'Are you ready to take up a new job from the first of next

month? You'll have to, I suppose, now that the bank is closing.'

'What did you say?' said Nathu.

'Haven't you heard? The bank's gone bankrupt. You'd better hang around until the others arrive, and then start demanding your money too. You'll be lucky if you get

it!' He waved cheerfully, and pedalled away on his bicycle.

Nathu went back to sweeping the steps, muttering to himself. When he had finished, he sat down on the bottom step to await the arrival of the manager. He was determined to get his pay.

'Who would have thought the bank would collapse,' he said to himself, and looked thoughtfully across the street. 'I wonder how it could have happened.'

The Thief's Story

I was still a thief when I met Romi. And though I was only fifteen years old, I was an experienced and fairly successful hand. Romi was watching a wrestling match when I approached him. He was about twenty-five and he looked easy-going, kind, and simple enough for my purpose. I was sure I would be able to win the young man's confidence. 'You look a bit of a wrestler yourself,' I said. There's nothing like flattery to break the ice!

'So do you,' he replied, which put me off for a moment because at that time I was rather thin and bony.

Well,' I said modestly, 'I do wrestle a bit.'

What's your name?'

'Hari Singh,' I lied. I took a new name every month, which kept me ahead of the police and former employers.

After these formalities Romi confined himself to commenting on the wrestlers, who were grunting, gasping, and heaving each other about. When he walked away, I followed him casually.

'Hello again,' he said.

I gave him my most appealing smile. 'I want to work for you,' I said.

'But I can't pay you anything—not for some time, anyway.'

I thought that over for a minute. Perhaps I had misjudged my man. 'Can you feed me?' I asked.

'Can you cook?'

'I can cook,' I lied again.

'If you can cook, then maybe I can feed you.'

He took me to his room over the Delhi Sweet Shop and told me I could sleep on the balcony. But the meal I cooked that night must have been terrible because Romi gave it to a stray dog and told me to be off.

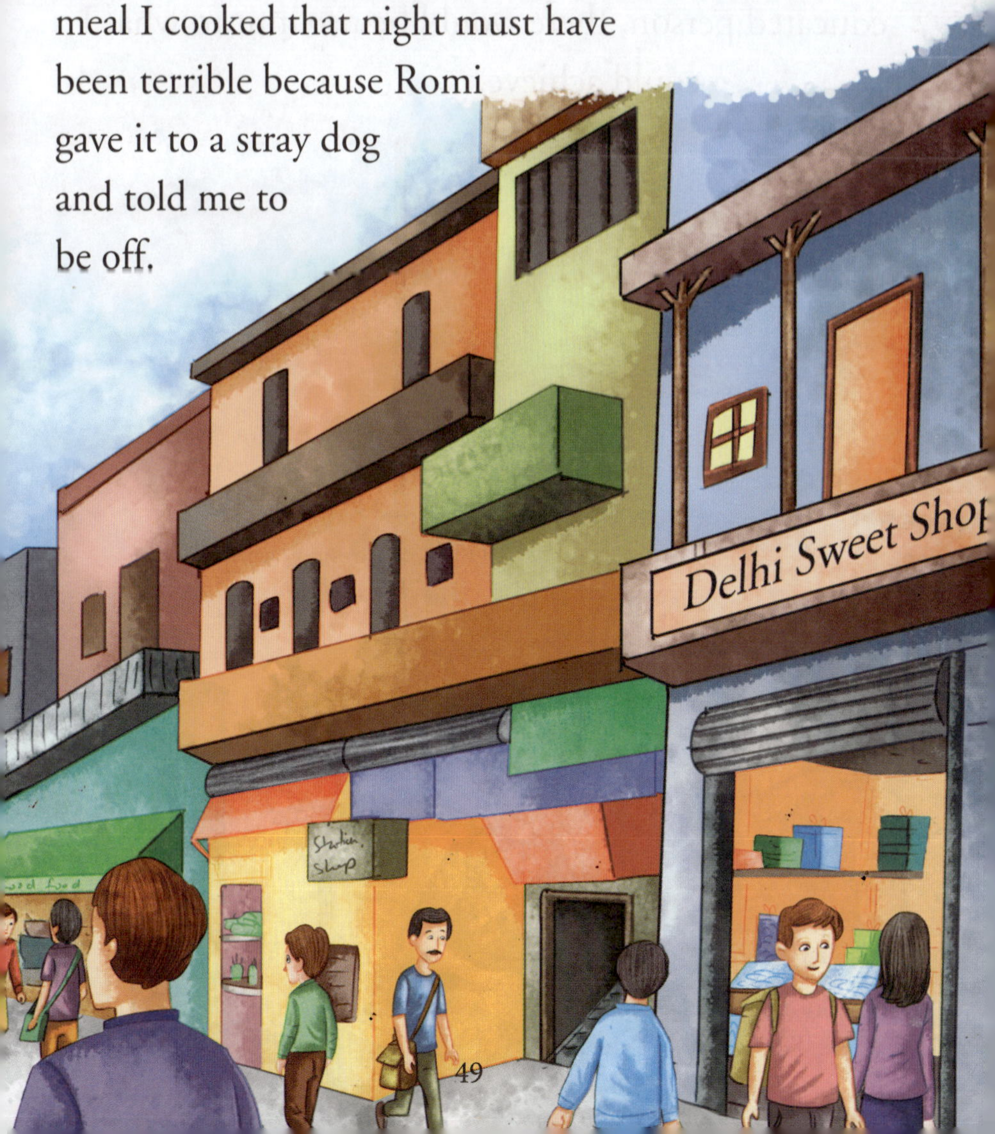

But I just hung around, smiling in my most appealing way, and he couldn't help laughing. Later, he patted me on the head and said, never mind, he'd teach me to cook. He also taught me to write my name and said he would soon teach me to write whole sentences and to add figures. I was grateful. I knew that once I could write like an educated person, there would be no limit to what I could achieve.

It was quite pleasant working for Romi. I made tea in the morning and then took my time buying the day's supplies, usually making a profit of two or three rupees. I think he knew I made a little money this way, but he didn't seem to mind.

Romi made money by fits and starts. He would borrow one week, lend the next. He kept worrying about his next cheque, but as soon as it arrived he would go out and celebrate. He wrote for the Delhi and Bombay magazines: a strange way to make a living.

One evening he came home with a small bundle of notes, saying he had just sold a book to a publisher. That night I saw him put the money in an envelope and tuck it under the mattress.

I had been working for Romi for almost a month and, apart from cheating on the shopping, had not done anything big in my real line of work. I had every opportunity for doing so. I could come and go as I pleased, and Romi was the most trusting person I had ever met.

That was why it was so difficult to rob him. It was easy for me to rob a greedy man. But robbing a nice man could be a problem. And if he doesn't notice he's being robbed, then all the spice goes out of the undertaking!

Well, it's time I got down to some real work, I told myself. If I don't take the money, he'll only waste it on his so-called friends. After all, he doesn't even give me a salary.

Romi was sleeping peacefully. A beam of moonlight reached over the balcony and fell on his bed. I sat on the floor, considering the situation. If I took the money, I could catch the 10.30 express to Lucknow. Slipping out of my blanket, I crept over to the bed. My hand slid under the mattress, searching for the notes. When I found the packet, I drew it out without a sound. Romi sighed in his sleep and turned on his side. Startled, I moved quickly out of the room.

Once on the road, I began to run. I had the money stuffed into a vest pocket under my shirt. When I'd gotten some distance from Romi's place, I slowed to a walk and, taking the envelope from my pocket, counted the money. Seven hundred rupees in fifties. I could live like a prince for a week or two!

When I reached the station, I did not stop at the ticket office (I had never bought a ticket in my life) but dashed straight on to the platform. The Lucknow Express was just moving out. The train had still to pick up speed and I should have been able to jump into one of the compartments, but I hesitated—for some reason I can't explain—and I lost the chance to get away.

When the train had gone, I found myself standing alone on the deserted platform. I had no idea where to spend the night. I had no friends, believing that friends were more trouble than help. And I did not want to arouse curiosity by staying at one of the small hotels nearby. The only person I knew really well was the man I had robbed. Leaving the station, I walked slowly through the bazaar.

In my short career, I had made a study of people's faces after they had discovered the loss of their valuables. The greedy showed panic; the rich showed anger; the poor, resignation. But I knew that Romi's face when he discovered the theft would show only a touch of

sadness—not for the loss of money, but for the loss of trust.

The night was chilly—November nights can be cold in northern India—and a shower of rain added to my discomfort. I sat down in the shelter of the clock tower. A few beggars and vagrants lay beside me, rolled up tight in their blankets. The clock showed midnight. I felt for the notes; they were soaked through.

Romi's money. In the morning, he would probably have given me five rupees to go to the movies, but now I had it all: no more cooking meals, running to the bazaar, or learning to write sentences.

Sentences! I had forgotten about them in the excitement of the theft. Writing complete sentences, I knew, could one day bring me more than a few hundred rupees. It was a simple matter to steal. But to be a really big man, a clever and respected man, was something else. I should go back to Romi, I told myself, if only to learn to read and write.

I hurried back to the room feeling very nervous, for it is much easier to steal something than to return it undetected.

I opened the door quietly, then stood in the doorway in clouded moonlight. Romi was still asleep. I crept to the head of the bed, and my hand came up with the packet of notes. I felt his breath on my hand. I remained still for a few moments. Then my fingers found the edge

of the mattress, and I slipped the money beneath it.

I awoke late the next morning to find that Romi had already made the tea. He stretched out a

hand to me. There was a fifty-rupee note between his fingers. My heart sank.

'I made some money yesterday,' he said. 'Now I'll be able to pay you regularly.'

My spirits rose. But when I took the note, I noticed that it was still wet from the night's rain.

So he knew what I'd done. But neither his lips nor his eyes revealed anything.

'Today we'll start writing sentences,' he said.

I smiled at Romi in my most appealing way. And the smile came by itself, without any effort.